Facts About

Ships

DONNA BAILEY

How to Use This Book

This book tells you many things about boats and ships. There is a Table of Contents on the next page. It shows you what each double page of the book is about. For example, pages 32 and 33 tell you about "Ocean Liners."

On all these pages you will find some words that are printed in **bold** type. The bold type shows you that these words are in the glossary on pages 46 and 47. The glossary explains the meaning of some words that may be new to you.

At the very end of the book there is an index. The index tells you where to find certain words in the book. For example, you can use it to look up words like rudder, paddle steamer, propeller.

Trade Edition published 1992 © Steck-Vaughn Company
Published in the United States in 1990 by Steck-Vaughn Co., **Austin, Texas,** a subsidiary of National Education Corporation.

© Macmillan Children's Books 1988
Artwork © BLA Publishing Limited 1988

All rights reserved. No reproduction, copy or transmission of this publication may be made without written permission.

Designed by Julian Holland

Printed and bound in the United States
2 3 4 5 6 7 8 9 0 LB 94

Library of Congress Cataloging-in-Publication Data

Bailey, Donna.
  Ships.

  (Facts about)
  Summary: Traces early maritime history from the Egyptians to Captain Cook, discusses how sails were developed to use the wind, describes clipper ships, steamships, ocean liners, working ships, inland waterways, and canals, and examines safety at sea and the future of ships.
  1. Ships—History—Juvenile literature. 2. Navigation—History—Juvenile literature. [1. Ships—History. 2. Navigation—History] I. Title. II. Series: Facts about (Austin, Tex.)
VM150.B25 1990   387.2   89-21727
ISBN 0-8114-2502-9 Hardcover Library Binding
ISBN 0-8114-6631-0 Softcover Binding

Contents

Introduction	4	Paddles and Propellers	28
How It All Began	6	Passage to America	30
The Egyptians	8	Ocean Liners	32
The Phoenicians	10	Ships at Work	34
The Vikings	12	Inland Waterways	36
Using the Wind	14	Canals	38
How Ships Changed	16	Giant Cargo Ships	40
Christopher Columbus	18	Safety at Sea	42
Around the World	20	New Kinds of Ships	44
James Cook	22		
Clipper Ships	24	Glossary	46
Steamships	26	Index	48

Introduction

Roads, railroads, and rivers all carry people and goods.

Our picture shows a road and a railroad running along the valley of the Rhine River in West Germany.

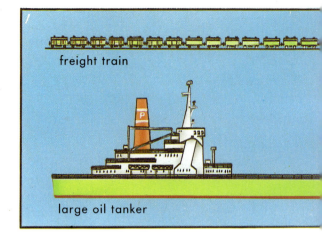

freight train

large oil tanker

Ships, planes, trains, and trucks all carry freight from one place to another.

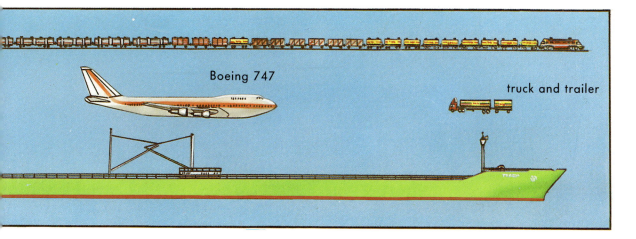

An oil tanker can carry more than a train but it is slower. A train can carry more than a truck and trailer.

Planes carry more than trains and are much faster.

People also use boats for fun and sport.

The sailing boat in our picture does not have an engine. It moves by the power of the wind.

which can carry the most?

a sailing boat

How It All Began

Long ago people did not have any boats. To cross a river, they probably sat on a log and paddled.

Later, people hollowed out the centers of long tree trunks to make **dugout** canoes.

paddling a log

dugout canoes are still used today

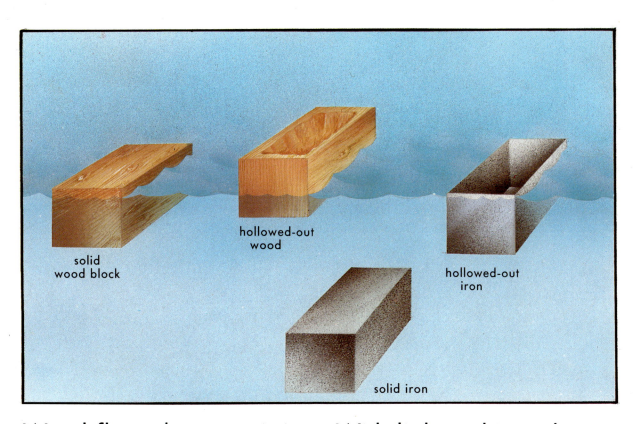

Wood floats because it is lighter than water, but a heavy block of iron will sink in the water. A hollow iron block is much lighter and will float, and a hollow block of wood floats even better.

If you put a stone in a full tub, some water will overflow.

With lighter things that float, the **displacement** of the water is less.

The Egyptians

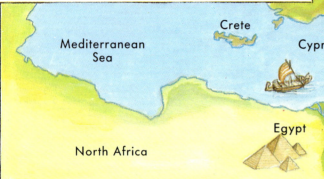

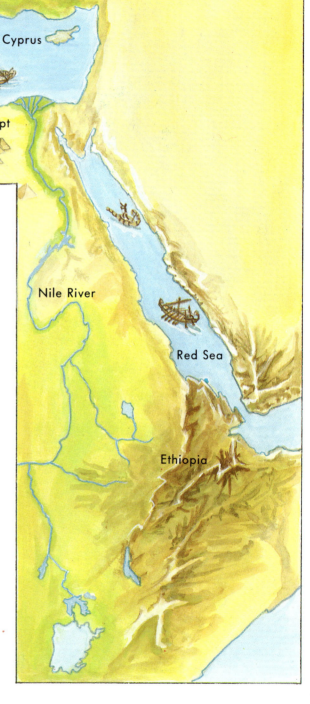

The first people to build real boats lived thousands of years ago in Egypt.

Our map shows Egypt, the Mediterranean Sea, the Red Sea, and the Nile River.

The Egyptians built their boats of wooden planks. Their boats also had **masts** and sails so that the winds could push them along.

Egyptian boats were curved at both ends. The sails were square and the masts were held in place by ropes.

The Egyptians used the paddle at the **stern** to steer the boat.

They sailed their boats up and down the Nile and across the sea to **trade** with other countries.

building the boat

an Egyptian boat

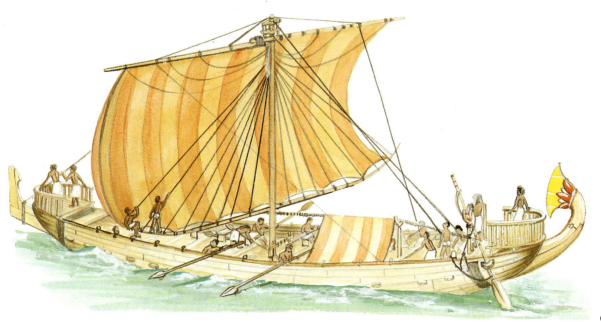

The Phoenicians

The Phoenicians built long warships with pointed **bows**, to **ram** other ships. Sails and oarsmen helped the ships to travel very fast.

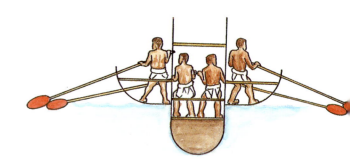

The Phoenicians were brave warriors, sailors, and explorers. They sailed around the Mediterranean Sea and all the way around Africa. They kept close to the coast and traded with people as they went.

Other traders sailed to England and northern Europe.

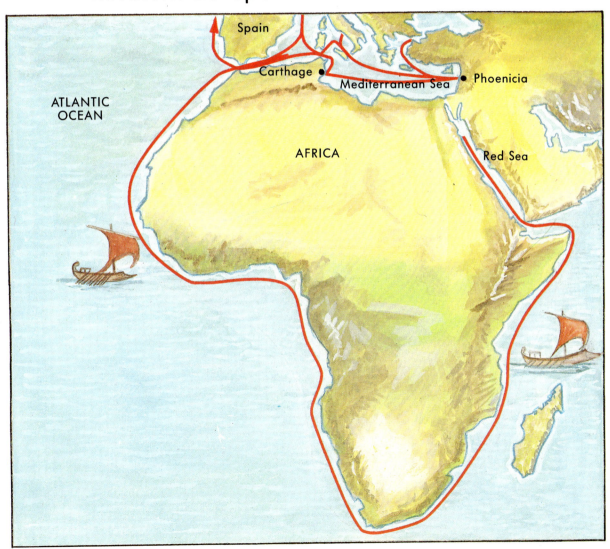

The Vikings

The Vikings were fierce warriors and good sailors who lived in northern Europe 1,000 years ago.
 Their ships were called longships and the Vikings used them for fighting and exploring other lands.

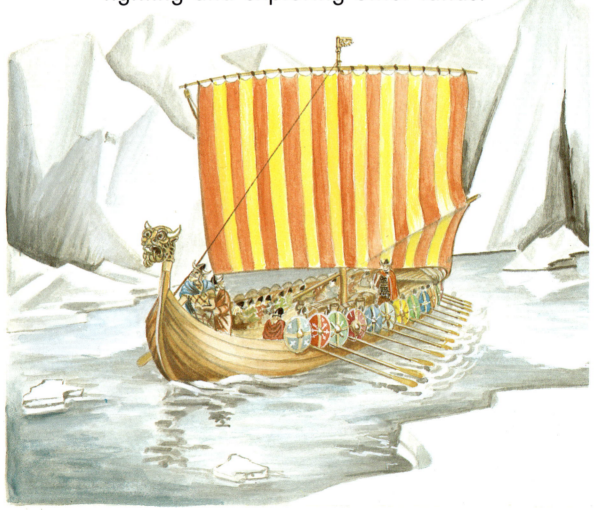

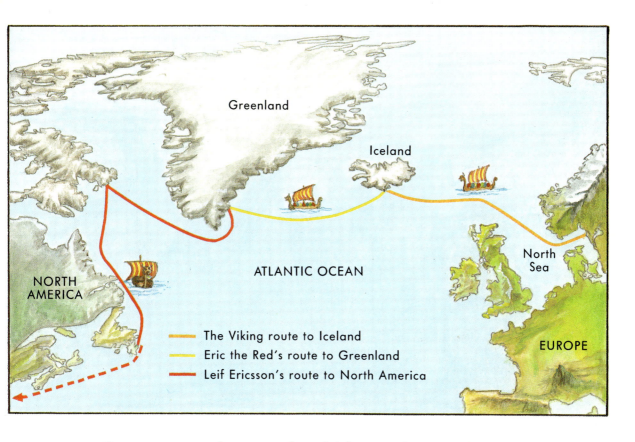

Our map shows the Vikings' journeys from northern Europe.

First they discovered Iceland and some Viking families settled there. Other sailors, like Eric the Red, sailed farther west and discovered Greenland.

Eric the Red settled in Greenland, but his son, Leif Ericsson, sailed on from Greenland and found a place that he called Vinland. Some people think it was New England.

Using the Wind

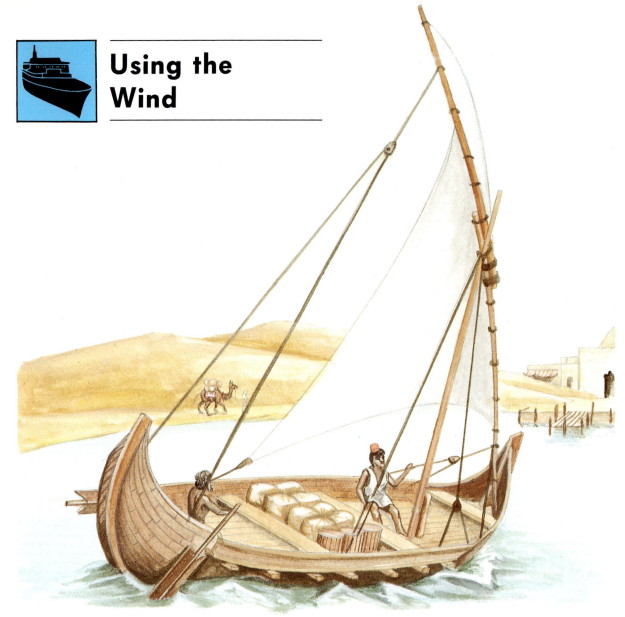

Arab seamen in the Red Sea were the first people to use triangular sails.
   This kind of sail is better than a square sail, which only works well if the wind is behind the boat. Triangular sails also work well when the wind blows across the boat.

Boats can move forward even when the wind is in front of the boat. To do this you have to **tack**. Each time the boat is turned, the sail moves across the boat to catch the wind so it fills the sails.

Following a Zigzag Course to Catch the Wind

direction of wind

direction of boat

How Ships Changed

People began to build bigger and stronger boats, with more masts and sails to give the ships more speed. Ships were built with a **rudder** at the stern to steer the boat, and "castles" at the bow and stern to protect the **crew**.

an early warship with a sail and oarsmen

a cog was a small merchant ship with "castles"

a Portuguese caravel had three sails

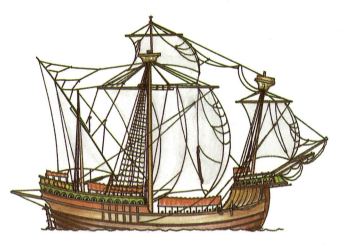

this galleass was the last warship with oarsmen and sails

this galleon had "castles" at the bow and stern

a Spanish galleon was used both for trading and war

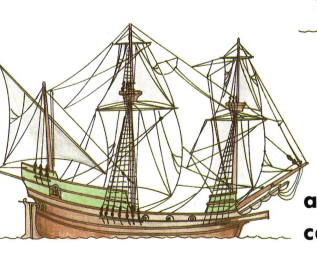

a large carrack could carry many passengers

Christopher Columbus

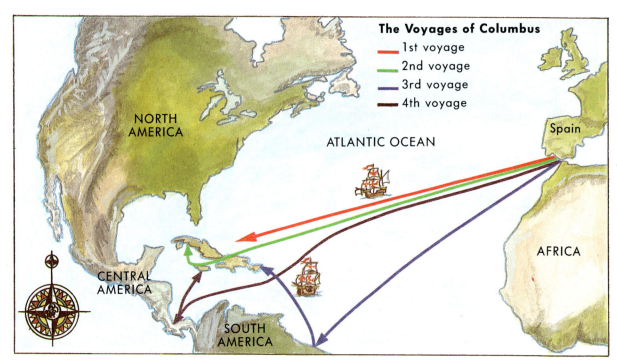

Our map shows the four voyages of the explorer, Christopher Columbus. His first voyage was in 1492 in his ship the *Santa Maria*, which was only about 115 feet long.

A large modern oil tanker is about ten times as long as the *Santa Maria*.

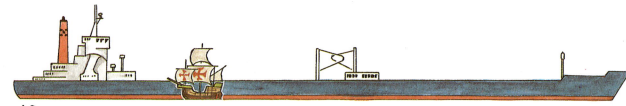

Below is a model of the *Santa Maria*. Columbus took 69 days to sail it across the Atlantic Ocean.

He thought he had sailed around the world to India, but he was wrong. He had landed in the West Indies.

On later journeys over the next ten years he went farther west. On his third and fourth voyages he landed at South America and Panama.

Around the World

Our map shows the voyages of other men who wanted to sail around the world.

In 1497 John Cabot got as far as Canada, which he thought was China.

In 1498 Vasco da Gama went east around Africa and landed in India.

In 1501 Amerigo Vespucci landed at places in South America. America was named after him.

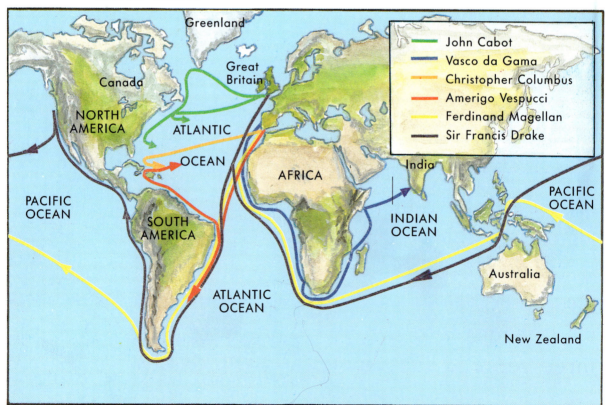

Magellan's ships

Ferdinand Magellan left Spain in 1519. His ships passed through the channel between the Atlantic and Pacific Oceans. Magellan was killed. Months later one of his captains arrived home with only one ship and 17 men.

Sir Francis Drake took three years to sail around the world.

Drake's ship, the *Golden Hind*

James Cook

Cook was the first person from Europe to discover Australia.
— 1st voyage
— 2nd voyage
— 3rd voyage

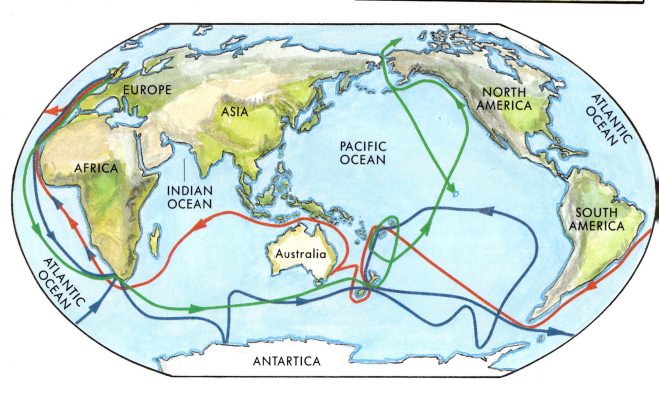

Captain James Cook was the first person from Europe to discover Australia. Our map shows the different voyages that he made.

In 1769 Captain Cook left England in his ship the *Endeavour*. He sailed west across the Atlantic and around Cape Horn into the Pacific. He explored Tahiti and New Zealand before he landed at Botany Bay on the east coast of Australia.

Cook was killed on his third voyage during a fight in Hawaii, in 1779.

Cook's ship, was very strong. He added two lower decks to the *Endeavour*, one deck for the crew, and the other to store food and drink.

Captain James Cook

Endeavour

Clipper Ships

Ships were needed to take settlers to the new lands and to bring back goods and produce.

Faster ships called **clippers** were built with big cargo **holds**. Clipper ships made trips to and from China carrying tea, passengers, and mail.

the *Pride of Baltimore*

the *Ann McKim*

Clippers used to race each other from China to London to bring back the new crop of tea.

Our picture shows the *Cutty Sark*, one of the most famous clipper ships, with its holds packed with tea.

The *Cutty Sark* also carried wool from Australia, in a record time of 69 days. The normal time for the journey was 100 days.

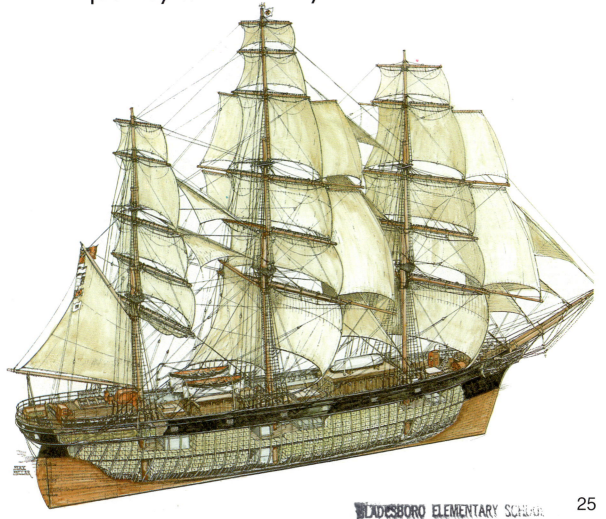

Steamships

The first steamships were used only on rivers, because they needed wood from the riverbanks to burn in their boilers.

In 1790, John Fitch ran the first steamship service up the Delaware River.

Fitch's ship, Experiment

Robert Fulton's ship, called the *Clermont*, had two paddle wheels and ran between New York and Albany.

the *Clermont* makes its first journey

At that time in America, the best way to travel was by river. So, many new paddle steamers were built. Some had wheels on either side of the **hull**, but others had huge wheels on the stern.

Our picture shows the paddle steamer *Delta Queen* at work on the Mississippi River.

Paddles and Propellers

Two steamships had a race across the Atlantic in 1838. On the way, one of them, the *Sirius*, ran out of fuel, so the crew burned all the furniture, doors, and planks to keep the boilers going.

the paddle steamer *Britannia*

In 1840 Samuel Cunard started a regular service of paddle steamers across the Atlantic. Our picture shows his paddle steamer *Britannia*.

In 1843 an engineer named Brunel built the *Great Western*, the first ship to have a **propeller**. The ship's engine turned the propeller. Our picture shows how a propeller's curved blades bite into the water and force the water backward so the ship moves forward.

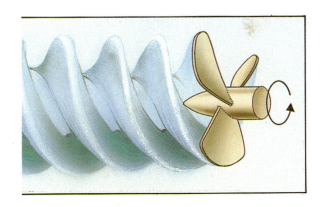

Passage to America

Our picture shows the cramped conditions below decks for the millions of poor people who came to find a better life in America.

Rich people traveled in cabins or open salons where they had more room to move about and they could have their food cooked for them. But crossing the Atlantic in the 1800s was still very dangerous, and many ships sank on the way over.

Ocean Liners

About 100 years ago Charles Parsons developed a new kind of steamship engine called a steam **turbine**. The turbine used less fuel and the ship could go faster, so soon all the Atlantic **shipping lines** began building bigger and faster ships. These new ocean **liners** were like huge hotels on water.

The *Queen Mary*, in our picture, crossed the Atlantic in under four days.

Today many ocean liners have been turned into **cruise ships**, like the *Queen Elizabeth II* in our picture.

New cruise liners in the future may look like this Norwegian model.

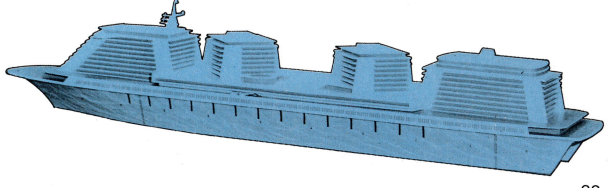

Ships at Work

Buses drive on a car ferry at one end and off at the other.

Our picture below shows a **crane** loading cargo onto a ship.

Our picture shows a busy harbor scene at Hong Kong.

The ship with the yellow funnel is an empty cargo ship, called a **freighter**.

The ship is high out of the water. The cargo is being loaded from the boats alongside it by cranes on the deck. The cranes are called **derricks**. There are also some **containers** on the dock waiting to be loaded.

Inland Waterways

Most countries have inland waterways of rivers and canals.

Our picture shows how a **lock** works. Locks help ships and **barges** go up and down the canals.

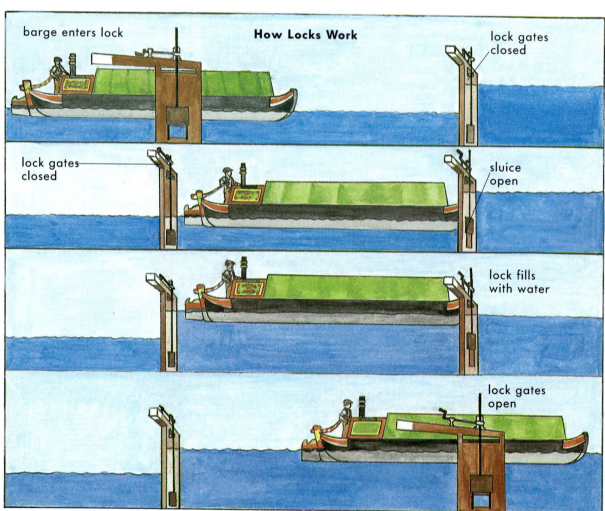

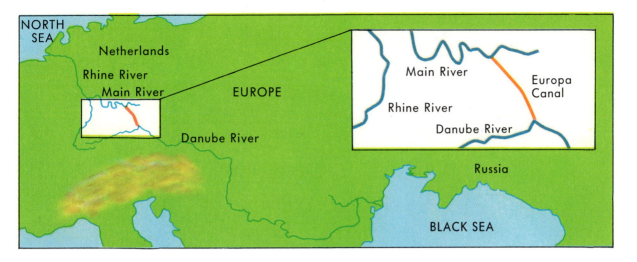

the Europa canal

rivers in North America

Countries are still building new canals to link up the waterways.

The Europa canal is being built to link the Danube River in Hungary with the Main River in Germany. Then ships can travel all the way from Russia to the Netherlands.

In America a canal links the Mississippi River with Chicago.

37

Canals

Our picture shows the Suez canal, which allows ships to travel from the Mediterranean to the Red Sea instead of going all the way around Africa. The Suez canal was dug out of the sandy desert.

The Panama canal is another important canal that links the Pacific and the Atlantic Oceans so that ships do not have to go all the way around South America.

Our map shows the St. Lawrence Seaway which is a great inland waterway that links the Great Lakes with the Atlantic.

the Panama canal

the St. Lawrence Seaway is shown in red

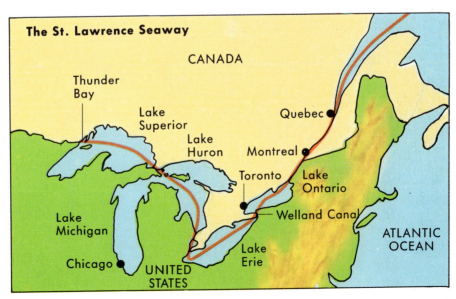

Giant Cargo Ships

Ships that carry only one kind of cargo are called **bulk carriers**.

An oil tanker, like the one in our picture, is a bulk carrier; it only carries oil in its holds.

Other ships have their cargo packed into containers.

Containers are all the same size and shape and fit very neatly into a ship's hold.

Our picture shows a container being loaded at a container terminal.

Safety at Sea

There are so many ships on the seas that they are equipped with **radar**. This shows the captain if there is another ship nearby so the ship can turn away to avoid a collision.

Our picture shows a ship's officer checking the radar screen. The radar screen lights up to show the position of other ships, rocks, and the coast.

Lighthouses warn ships where there are dangerous rocks near the coast.

The **coast guard** also checks the movement of ships, and if a ship is in trouble, they send out a lifeboat to rescue the crew.

New Kinds of Ships

The hydrofoil is one of the new kinds of ships that we use today. When the hydrofoil leaves the harbor and gathers speed, the foils under its bow lift the boat out of the water.

This ship can travel very fast because it is nearly out of the water.

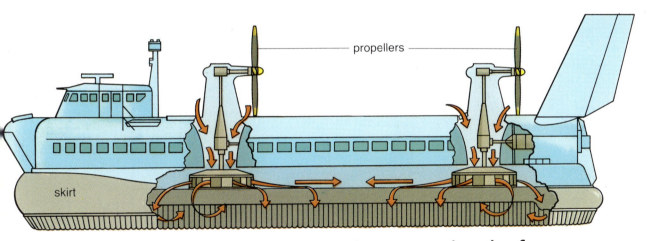

The hovercraft is another new kind of ship, which floats on a cushion of air. When the hovercraft leaves the harbor, air is pumped into the "skirt," and the hovercraft is lifted above the water.

Glossary

barge a flat-bottomed boat built to carry cargo on rivers and canals.
bow the front end of a boat or ship.
bulk carrier a large ship that carries a single kind of cargo.
clipper a long, narrow sailing ship built for speed. Clippers carried people and cargo over long distances.
coast guard a group of service people who watch the shores of a country and aid ships or people in trouble.
container a large metal box for carrying cargo.
crane a machine for lifting heavy objects.
crew the captain, officers, and sailors on a ship.
cruise ships ships that take people for vacation voyages.
derrick a crane on the deck of a ship, used to lift cargo in and out of the hold.
displacement the amount of water forced out of place when an object is put into the water.
dugout a simple boat made by hollowing out a tree trunk.
freighter a cargo vessel, powered by an engine.
hold the part of a ship where goods and cargo are carried.
hull the main body or shell of a ship.
liner a ship carrying passengers, that makes regular voyages at fixed times.
lock a stretch of canal with gates at each end. The gates are closed at one end, and a ship enters the canal through the open gates at the other end. These gates are then closed and the water level is raised or lowered in the lock to match the water level on the other side, and so allows the ship to go up or down the canal easily.
mast the tall pole that holds the sails aloft.
propeller a propeller is made of two twisted blades. As it turns it pushes the ship forward.
radar a way of finding the position of an object. Radio

waves are sent out. When they meet an object, they bounce back to the radar set and show up as points of light on the screen.

ram to hit and sink an enemy ship with a heavy piece of wood attached to the bow of a warship.

rudder a hinged flat piece of wood used to steer boats or planes.

shipping lines companies that organize the regular sailing of ships according to set timetables.

stern the rear of a ship.

tack sailing on a zigzag course.

trade selling goods and produce in exchange for money or other goods.

turbine a shaft with many curved blades on it. Steam makes the turbine shaft turn around. It drives a ship's propeller.

Index

boilers 28
bow 10, 16
Britannia 29
Brunel, 29
bulk carriers 40
cabins 31
Cabot, John 20
canals, 36, 37
car ferry 34
cargo 24, 25, 34, 35, 40
Clermont 26
clippers 24, 25
coast guard 43
Columbus, 18, 19
container terminals 40
Cook, James 22, 23
crew 16, 28, 43
cruise ships 33
Cunard, Samuel 29
Cutty Sark 25

da Gama, Vasco 20
Delta Queen 27

displacement 7
Drake, Francis 21
dugout canoes 6

Endeavour 22, 23
Eric the Red 13
Ericsson, Leif 13
explorers 11, 12, 18, 20, 21, 22, 23

Fitch, John 26
freighter 35
Fulton, Robert 26

Golden Hind 21
Great Western 29

holds 24, 25, 40
hovercraft 45
hydrofoil 44

lifeboat 43
liners 32, 33
locks 36
longships 12

Magellan, 21
masts 8, 9, 16

oarsmen 10
oil tanker 5, 18

paddle 9
paddle steamers 27, 29

Panama canal 39
Parsons, Charles 32
propeller, 29

Queen Elizabeth II 33
Queen Mary 32

radar 42
rivers 4, 26, 36
rudder 16

sailing boat 5
sailors 11, 12
sails 8, 9, 10, 14, 15, 16
Santa Maria 18, 19
shipping lines 32
Sirius 28
St. Lawrence Seaway 39
steamships 26, 28, 32
stern 9, 16
Suez canal 38

tack 15
turbines 32

Vespucci, Amerigo 20

warships 10
wind 5, 8, 14, 15

Acknowledgments
The Publishers wish to thank the following organizations for their invaluable assistance in the preparation of this book:
Boeing Company; British Caledonian; British Hovercraft Corporation; British Petroleum; Norwegian Caribbean Lines; Racal-Decca Company; Royal National Lifeboat Institution; University of Liverpool

Photographic credits (*t = top b = bottom l = left r = right*)
4b ZEFA; 5b Yachting World; 7b Philip Sauvain; 19 "Trustees of the Science Museum" (London); 21t The Mansell Collection; 21b National Maritime Museum London; 23t The Mansell Collection; 23b National Maritime Museum London; 24t ZEFA; 24b Mystic Seaport Museum; 27 ZEFA; 29t, 32 University of Liverpool; 33t British Caledorian; 33b Norwegian Caribbean Lines; 34t, 34b, 35, 38, 39n ZEFA; 40 British Petroleum, 41 ZEFA; 42 Racal-Decca Company; 43t ZEFA; 43b Royal National Lifeboat Institution; 44 Boeing Company; 45t British Hovercraft Corporation; Cover photograph; Colorific/Robert Wright. Title page Colorific/J. Allan Cash.